A Beginning-to-Read Book

W9-AWZ-827

Where is Dear Dragon?

by Margaret Hillert

Illustrated by David Schimmell

NORWOOD HOUSE PRESS

The **Dear Dragon** series is comprised of carefully written books that extend the collection of classic readers you may remember from your own childhood. Each book features text focused on common sight words. Through the use of controlled text, these books provide young children with abundant practice recognizing the words that appear most frequently in written text. Rapid recognition of high-frequency words is one of the keys for developing automaticity which, in turn, promotes accuracy and rate necessary for fluent reading. The many additional details in the pictures enhance the story and offer opportunities for students to expand oral language and develop comprehension.

Shannon Cannon

Shannon K. Cannon, Ph.D.
Literacy Consultant

Norwood House Press • P.O. Box 316598 • Chicago, Illinois 60631
For more information about Norwood House Press please visit our website at *www.norwoodhousepress.com* or call 866-565-2900.

Text copyright ©2013 by Margaret Hillert. Illustrations and cover design copyright ©2013 by Norwood House Press, Inc. All rights reserved. No part of this book may be reproduced or utilized in any form or by any means without written permission from the publisher.

This book was manufactured as a paperback edition. If you are purchasing this book as a rebound hardcover or without any cover, the publisher and any licensors' rights are being violated.

Paperback ISBN: 978-1-60357-449-5

The Library of Congress has cataloged the original hardcover edition with the following call number: 2012012630

© 2013 by Norwood House Press. All Rights Reserved. No part of this book may be reproduced without written permission from the publisher.
This paperback edition was published in 2013.

Printed in ShenZhen, Guangdong, China.
297R–092016.

Where are you, Dear Dragon?
Are you in this little red house?
Come out.
Come out.

No, you are not there.
Mother. Mother.
I cannot find Dear Dragon.
Where can he be?

I did not see him.
You will have to look for him.

Here I go.
Oh, oh.
I can look for Dragon in this big box.

7

Look here.
Here is my blue ball.

And here is a red bat.
And a yellow hat.
But— no Dear Dragon!

I can look in here, too.
Is Dragon in here?
I want that dragon.

No, no.
He is not in here.
Where can he be?

Now there is a spot.
I will look there.
Will I find him there?

No, no Dragon.

Out. Out.
Now I will go out to look for Dragon.

Are you out here now?
Did you come out here?
I want you.

Are you in here, Dragon?
Did you get into the car?
No, I guess not.

Did Mother find Dragon for me?
I will go and see.
I will go into the house and see.

No I did not see Dragon.

Oooohhh! Did you go down here?
Come up. Come up.

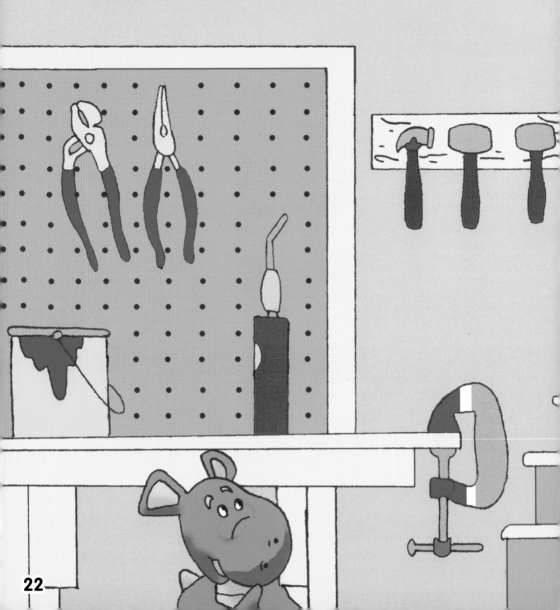

I cannot find Dragon.

Mother. Mother.
I cannot find Dragon.
Did you find him for me?

Come here now.
We have work to do.
You can make the bed.

Oh, Oh.
What is this?
What is in my bed?

27

YOU!
Here you are Dragon.
You are in my bed!

Now here you are with me.
And here I am with you.
What a funny, funny dear dragon.

WORD LIST

Where is Dear Dragon? uses the 64 words listed below.
This list can be used to practice reading the words that appear in the text.
You may wish to write the words on index cards and use them to help your
child build automatic word recognition. Regular practice with these words
will enhance your child's fluency in reading connected text.

a	dear	I	see
am	did	in	spot
and	down	into	
are	dragon	is	that
			the
ball	find	little	there
be	for	look	this
bed	funny		to
big		make	too
blue	get	me	
box	go	mother	up
but	guess	my	
			want
can	hat	no	we
cannot	have	not	what
car	he	now	where
come	here		will
	him	oh	with
	house	out	work
		red	yellow

ABOUT THE AUTHOR Margaret Hillert has written over 80 books for children who are just learning to read. Her books have been translated into many different languages and over a million children throughout the world have read her books. She first started writing poetry as a child and has continued to write for children and adults throughout her life. A first grade teacher for 34 years, Margaret is now retired from teaching and lives in Michigan where she likes to write, take walks in the morning, and care for her three cats.

Photograph by Glenna Washburn

ABOUT THE ADVISOR Shannon K. Cannon is a teacher educator, staff developer, and curriculum writer. She earned her doctorate in Language, Literacy, and Culture from the University of California Davis, where she serves on their clinical faculty supervising pre-service teachers, teaching elementary methods courses in reading/language arts and technology, and teaching Master's courses in inquiry. She began her career teaching second grade. She then spent over 15 years in educational publishing where her work included developing and writing curricular programs as well as providing professional development support to classroom teachers.

ABOUT THE ILLUSTRATOR David Schimmell served as a professional firefighter for 23 years before hanging up his boots and helmet to devote himself to working as an illustrator of children's books. David has happily created illustrations for the New Dear Dragon books as well as the artwork for educational and retail book projects. Born and raised in Evansville, Indiana, he lives there today with his wife and family.